# Little Penguin's Big Adventure

igloobooks

Little Penguin was bored with making friends out of snow.

"I'll just sit here and wait for something exciting to happen," he said.

So, Little Penguin waited and waited, but nothing happened at all.

Suddenly, a seagull swooped down. "You need to find Adventure," he said. "Where's Adventure?" asked the puzzled penguin. The seagull pointed to a small, red boat, bobbing on the sea. "I think it's that way," he replied.

SQUAWK!

On the small, red boat, Little Penguin asked the captain a question. "Do you know the way to Adventure?" The captain twiddled his whiskers. "I think it's that way," he said, pointing to a distant desert island.

**WHOOOO !** went the wind, as the waves lapped and slapped at the small, red boat.

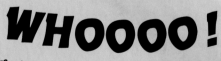

**WHOOOO !**
it went again, as the great sea swelled and rolled.

Soon, Little Penguin felt very, very sick.

Little Penguin hopped off the small, red boat at a desert island.
"Shiver me timbers!" cried a fierce pirate captain and his mad pirate crew,
who happened to be passing. "He's after our treasure!"

"I'm just trying to find Adventure," replied Little Penguin. "Can you show me the way, please?"

"Arrr, it be that way," said the pirate captain, swishing his cutlass to point at his ship.

On the pirate ship, there was a lot of swabbing the decks, eating cookies and sailing the Seven Seas. "But where is Adventure?" asked Little Penguin. "It be that way," said the crafty captain, pointing to a plank that poked out to sea.

Little Penguin walked along the plank until...

## ...SPLASH!

Down, down he went, to the bottom of the sea, but he wasn't alone.

"Hellooo," said a shark, with his best sharky smile.

"Err, do you know the way to Adventure?" asked Little Penguin, nervously.

"Go that way," replied the shark. "But you had better be quick!"

SNAP,
SNAP,
SNAP!

Little Penguin swam as fast as he could.
He darted and dashed under the coral, over the reef,
behind the rocks and **WHOOSH!** out of the sea...

**WHEE!** into a tree. Oo-oo! went some silly monkeys swinging by. "Do you know where I can find Adventure?" asked Little Penguin.

"Oh, yes," replied the naughty monkeys, **OO-OO-OOING** and making a racket. "It's that way," they said, pointing to a bush.

The bush was quiet, there was hardly a sound. Only the leaves
rustled and the parrots squawked and it was very, very still until...
...**ROAR!** went the lion who was hiding there.

Little Penguin ran and ran as fast as he could, through the trees, by the waterhole and down the hill.

There were hisses and **SNAPS** and **SNORTS** and **SQUAWKS!**

"Which way to Adventure?" cried Little Penguin, as he sped past the flamingos. "I think it's that way," said the flamingo leader, pointing to a sail boat.

Little Penguin jumped into the boat and sailed off down the river. The river grew wider and became the ocean and before too long, a great storm came.

Poor Little Penguin was all alone.

"I don't want to find Adventure any more!" cried Little Penguin
and he began to cry. He missed his mommy and daddy. He missed
being bored and sitting on his rock and twiddling his flippers.
"I want to go home!" he sobbed.

Just then, a great whale sprayed seawater from his spout.

SWOOSH!

"Don't cry, Little Penguin," he said. "I know exactly
where home is," and he pointed to an iceberg far, far away.
So, Little Penguin jumped on his back and off they went.

At home, his mommy and daddy were waiting on the shore.
"Where have you been, Little Penguin?" they asked. "It's nearly bedtime."
Little Penguin told them all about the places he had been.
"It sounds like you found Adventure," said Dad.